Other books illustrated by Bernadette Watts
and published by North-South Books:

Little Red Riding Hood
Hansel and Gretel
Snow White
Snow White and Rose Red
The Elves and the Shoemaker
The Bremen Town Musicians
Rumpelstiltskin
The Brave Little Tailor
The Snow Queen
Thumbelina
The Fir Tree
Varenka
George's Garden
Tattercoats
The Four Good Friends
The Wind and the Sun
Shoemaker Martin
The Little Donkey
Trouble at Christmas
Fly away, Fly away over the Sea
Goldilocks and the Three Bears

First published in Switzerland under the title *Der Hirsebrei*

First published in Great Britain, Canada,
Australia and New Zealand in 1994 by North-South Books,
an imprint of Nord-Süd Verlag AG, Gossau Zürich, Switzerland.

British Library Cataloguing in Publication Data is available

ISBN 1 55858 300 9

1 3 5 7 9 10 8 6 4 2

Printed in Belgium

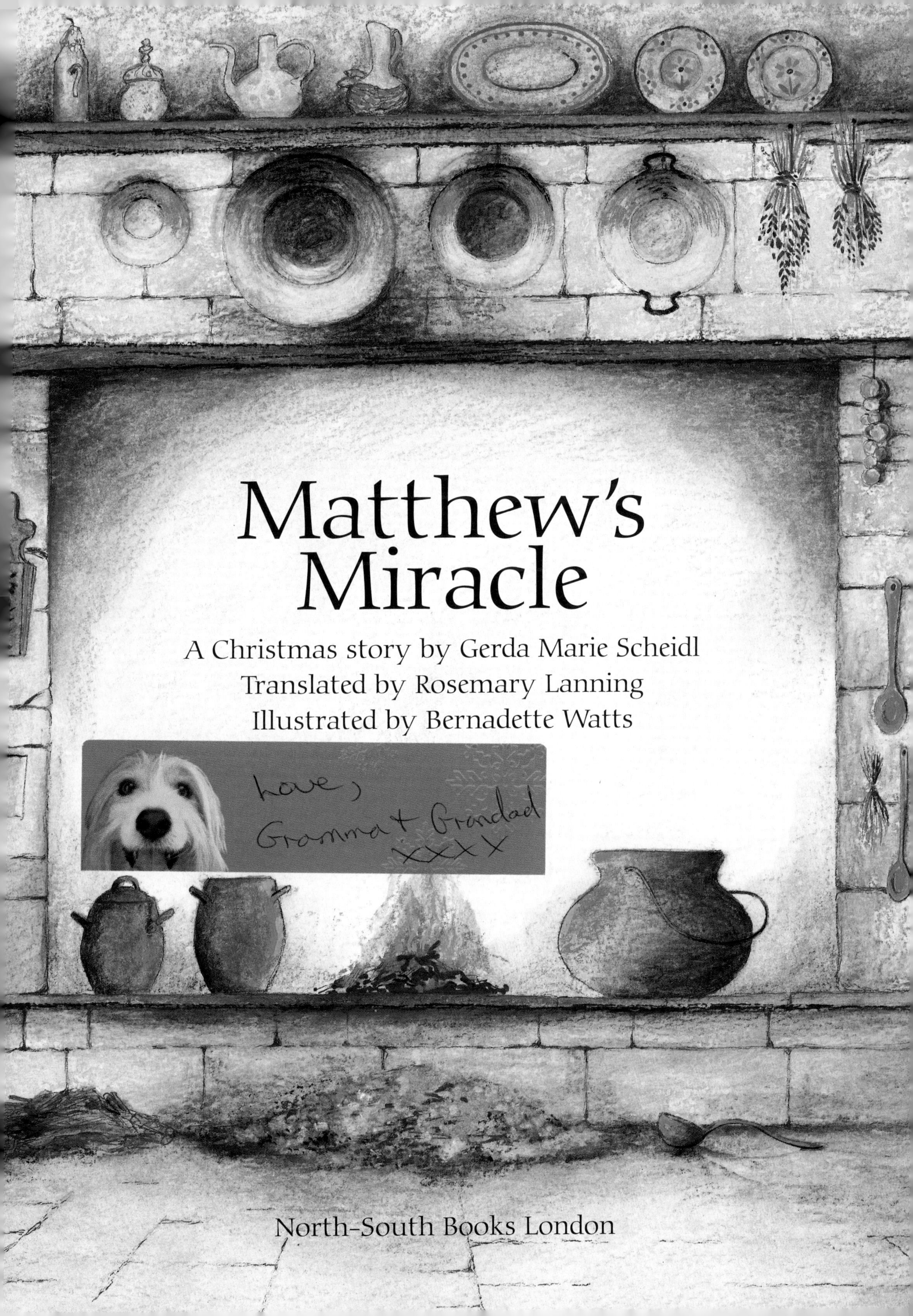

Matthew's Miracle

A Christmas story by Gerda Marie Scheidl
Translated by Rosemary Lanning
Illustrated by Bernadette Watts

North-South Books London

"Who are those people?" asked Matthew, having watched his father lead a man and a woman to the stable behind the inn. The innkeeper didn't reply. He was in no mood for questions. The inn was full and he had wanted to turn the man and his wife away, but then he had felt sorry for them. The woman looked tired and ill. With luck, he thought, they would keep themselves to themselves out there in the stable, and not give him any trouble.

"Tell me about those people," Matthew insisted as his father bustled in and out of the kitchen.

"Just penniless travellers," said his father impatiently. "That's all you need to know."

"Why didn't you let them come into the house?" asked Matthew. "They could have slept in my room."

"And where would you sleep, my son? In the stable?"

"Yes, why not?" said Matthew.

"No son of mine sleeps in a stable with the animals," said his father.

"Now," said the innkeeper, "I'll have no more questions. I've more than enough to do, with so many guests in the house. Stop worrying about those people in the stable and go and help your mother cook the porridge."

"May I take a bowl of warm porridge to the people in the stable, Father?"

"Certainly not! There's barely enough to feed the guests. By the time they've all eaten there won't be a spoonful left over."

Mother will give those poor people something to eat, thought Matthew, but his mother was too busy to listen to him.

"Ask me later," she said. "I can't stop and talk. I have too many guests to feed. Come and stir this porridge for me."

Night fell, and all was quiet at the inn, but still Matthew could not sleep. Outside, the light seemed far too bright.
Matthew drew back his curtain, knelt at the window and gazed in wonder at the dazzling star which now stood directly over the stable.

What could this mean? He must run to the stable and find out.

But when he reached the stable, Matthew stopped and dared not go in.

He saw the woman cradling a baby in her arms. Beside her stood the man, looking down lovingly at his wife and child.

As Matthew stood and stared, shepherds came to the stable.

"Why are you standing out here?" they asked. "Did you not hear the angels sing? Have you not heard their news of the infant king, born in a stable?"

Timidly, Matthew followed the shepherds into the stable and saw them kneel before the newborn child. Then he looked at the mother and saw how pale and weak she was. He remembered how tenderly everyone had cared for his own mother after his sister was born. She had lain in bed, wrapped in warm blankets, for three days and his father had brought her porridge mixed with egg to help her regain her strength.

Porridge! Of course! There must be some porridge left in the pot. Matthew ran back to the inn. He fetched two eggs, stirred them into the leftover porridge, then carried the heavy pot to the stable.

As the woman began to eat, colour returned to her cheeks and she smiled gratefully at Matthew. He wanted to smile back, but then he thought how angry his father would be when he found the pot empty. Terrified, Matthew ran back to bed, leaving the cooking pot where it lay.

When Matthew woke, his father was standing over him, looking very angry indeed. "Where is the cooking pot?" he asked. "Have you disobeyed me and given porridge to those people in the stable?"

Matthew jumped out of bed. "I'll get it back," he stammered and fled from the room.

How could he explain the empty pot? Matthew was sure his father would beat him when he saw that all the porridge was gone.

When Matthew came into the stable, the man and woman were asleep, but the baby was wide awake. Calmly, he returned Matthew's gaze, and suddenly Matthew was no longer afraid.

He picked up the empty pot to carry it back to the house, and was amazed at how heavy it was.

The cooking pot seemed to grow heavier and heavier. Matthew was glad to put it down again in the kitchen.

His father looked into the pot. "You are lucky there is still some porridge left," he said, sounding less angry now.

"But there is much more in the pot than last night!" exclaimed his mother.

Matthew looked into the pot and all he could say was, "O-o-oh!" The pot was full to the brim.

"Did you take porridge from the store-room, Matthew?" asked his father sternly.

Matthew shook his head, and was just about to tell his father all the miraculous things that had happened in the night when a crowd of hungry guests burst into the kitchen, demanding food.

"Be patient!" said the innkeeper. "Today there is more than enough for everyone."

And so there was. When at last the guests went away, satisfied, Matthew began his story, anxiously watching his father's face to see if he would be punished for his disobedience. "Please don't be angry," he said, finally.

"No, what you did was right," said his mother, and his father nodded in agreement.

"Never again will I turn tired and hungry people away from my door," he said. "You and the miraculous cooking pot have shown me what to do."